Dysgraphia

Writing Practice

Workbook for Kids

Ages 8-10

This Book Belongs To:

ISBN: 978-1-965964-00-2

Table of Contents

Enjoying this Book?

We'd love to hear your thoughts

We may just send you something special.

A Note to Parents

Thank you for choosing our **Dysgraphia Writing Practice Workbook for Kids Ages 8–10**. This book was designed to support children who learn differently and to give them the tools they need to grow into confident, capable writers. Every activity has been created with dysgraphic learners in mind so that writing feels clear, enjoyable, and achievable.

This workbook focuses on phonics, spelling, grammar, sentence writing, and creative expression, which are all important building blocks for writing success. You can support your child by reading instructions aloud when needed, practicing words and writing prompts together, and praising their effort as much as their accuracy.

We encourage you to approach each page with patience and positivity. Some activities may feel simple while others may take more time, and that is perfectly normal. The goal is not to finish quickly but to build writing skills and confidence step by step.

Remember that every child's learning journey is unique. With encouragement, consistent practice, and the right tools, your child will continue to grow and succeed. We are excited to be part of that journey with you.

Writing & Coloring Mini-Book

5 fun stories with questions and coloring activities designed for dyslexic learners. Build fluency and confidence while making reading fun!

Audio Included!

QR Code in the Back of the Book

For Kids Only

This book was made to help you have fun while you practice writing. Inside, you will find activities like handwriting practice, word building, sentence starters, story prompts, and creative exercises that will help you express your ideas, improve your spelling and grammar, and grow your confidence as a writer.

Each page is clear and simple so you can focus on writing without feeling rushed. You will also find fun doodles to color on every page. Grab your favorite crayons, markers, or colored pencils and make the doodles your own. Writing can be even more fun when you color while you learn.

Sometimes the pages will feel easy, and other times they may feel a little tricky. That is okay. Every time you practice, you are becoming a stronger writer.

Writing is not only about putting words on paper. It is about practicing your skills, using your imagination, sharing your thoughts, and enjoying the journey of creating something new.

Unit ①

Activity 1 — What Do You Hear?

Instructions: Say the name of the picture out loud. Write ✎ the beginning letter sound to complete the name of the picture.

1

_____pple

4

_____urtle

2

_____ion

5

_____ish

3

_____at

6

_____ee

Instructions Say the name of the picture.
Write ✎ the missing final letter to complete the word.

1

lio___

2

elephan___

3

koal___

4

zebr___

5

fo___

6

tige___

Blend It Like a Word Star

Instructions Blend the phonemes below to create a word. Write ✍ the word. Then, draw ✏ and color ✏ the picture.

🚀 A phoneme is a sound.

Phoneme (Sounds)	Write ✍ the word.	Draw ✏ and color ✏ the picture.
1 /s/ + /u/ + /n/		
2 /b/ + /a/ + /t/		
3 /m/ + /a/ + /p/		
4 /r/ + /a/ + /t/		
5 /c/ + /u/ + /p/		

Instructions

Look at the picture. Say the word out loud. Now break the word into its sounds. With the use of your crayons, write ✎ one sound in each box following the color code provided below.

Color Code

beginning sound (green)   middle sound (orange)

final sound (blue)

1 

4 

2 

5 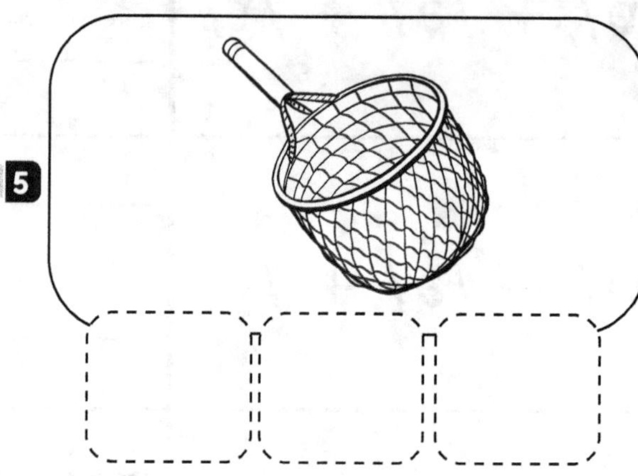

3 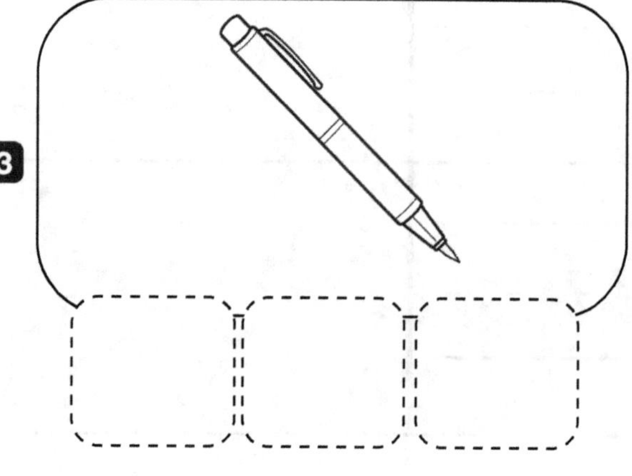

6 

Instructions

Read 👓 the word and circle the silent letter.
Color ✏️ the picture that matches the word.
Then, use the word in a sentence.

🚀 Some letters are quiet, but they still count!

WORD	PICTURE	SENTENCE
knife		__________
gnome		__________
wrist	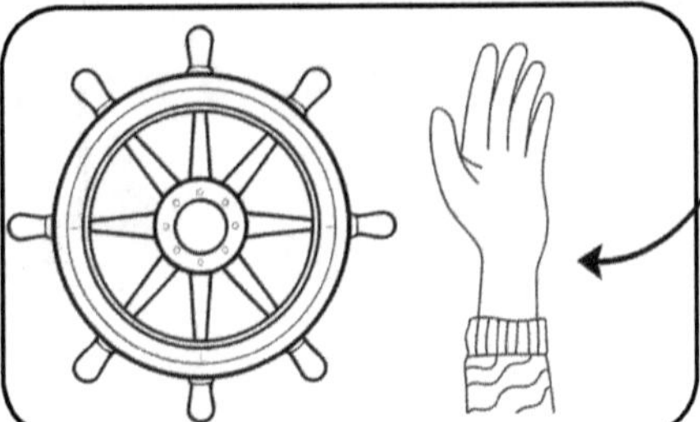	__________
thumb		__________
ghost		__________

Instructions

Draw a line to connect the words that sound the same (words that rhyme).

Words can be besties too, especially when they sound the same!

1 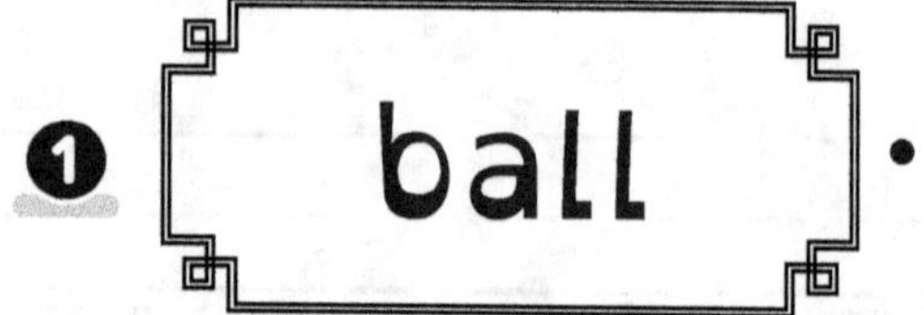 ball • •  rug

2  cat • • 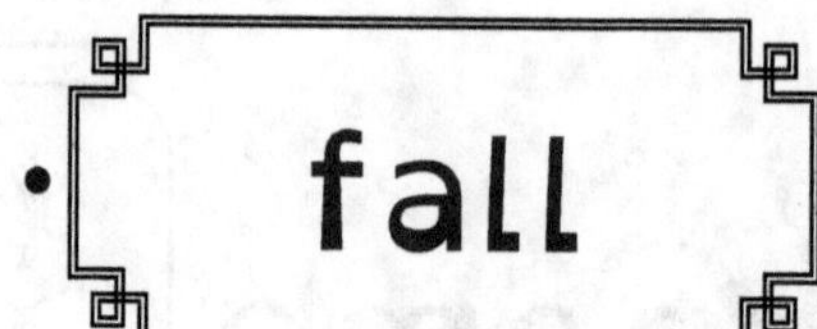 fall

3  bug • •  bee

4  light • • hat

5  tree • • kite

Activity **7** — Sound-Fix Sentences

Instructions Use the word bank to fill in the blanks with the correct word. Then rewrite ✐ the complete sentence on the line provided.

🚀 The sounds are hiding, can you find the right one?

Word Bank

cat   book   rain   hand   look

1 My _____________ chased a toy.

____

____

2 I held your _____________ tightly.

____

____

3 I read a good _____________ at bedtime.

____

____

4 I love the sound of the _____________.

____

____

5 Please take a _____________ at the board.

____

____

Instructions Fix the tricky word by writing ✎ the correct spelling and use the word in a sentence.

🚀 Some spellings are sneaky, let's straighten them out!

WORD	CORRECT WORD	SENTENCE
1  frend		
2 skool		
3 wurld		
4 fone		
5 fite		

Instructions Circle the word that matches the picture you see.

Say it. Hear it. Choose the word that sounds just right!

1 

try   tree   tray

4 

horse   house   harsh

2 

bay   buy   bee

5 

right   rite   write

3 

deer   dare   door

6 

knight   night   nayt

Instructions Read 👓 each sentence. Circle ○ the word that's spelled wrong or used the wrong way. Then, rewrite ✎ the sentence correctly on the line.

 Some sentences just don't sound quite right... Can you make them better?

1 He weared a red cap.

2 They runned to the park.

3 I seed a frog by the pond.

4 We eated lunch at noon.

5 He drawed a big dinosaur.

SYLLABLE AWARENESS

Unit ②

Activity 1 — Clap It Out: Syllable Superstars

Instructions Say the word out loud and clap once for each syllable. Count the claps, then sort the words based on how many syllables they have and write ✎ them on their corresponding columns.

A syllable is a beat or sound part in a word. Every time your chin drops or you clap when you say a word, that's one syllable!

Word Bank

sun	banana	carrot	jet	cupcake
monkey	zoo	butterfly	candy	elephant

1 Syllable	2 Syllables	3 Syllables

Break It to Make It

Instructions Read 👓 the word. Break each word into syllables and write ✏ it with dashes. Use the word in a sentence.

🚀 Big words are easier when you break them into pieces!

WORD	BREAK DOWN OF SYLLABLES	SENTENCE
calculator		
cupcake		
watermelon		
sister		
banana		

Instructions Draw a line to connect the first part of each word to the correct ending.

Let's snap those word pieces together like puzzle parts!

1 cup-

2 but-

3 win-

4 mon-

5 spi-

-ter

-key

-cake

-dow

-der

Instructions Read 👓 the clue. Fill in the missing syllables to complete the correct word. Then, use the word to create sentences.

🚀 Every word needs all its parts—can you find what's missing?

1 I'm something you drink every day. _ _ _ _ **ter**

2 I fly with colorful wings. **butter** _ _ _

3 You eat me with syrup for breakfast. _ _ _ _ **cake**

4 I open to let in fresh air. _ **win** _ _ _

5 I swing from trees and love bananas! _ _ _ **key**

Activity 5 — Syllable Scramble

Instructions Rebuild the words from these scrambled syllables. Write the correct word, then draw the picture.

Uh-oh! These syllables got mixed up... Can you put them back in the right order?

SCRAMBLED WORDS	CORRECT WORD	DRAW THE PICTURE.
ground-play		
na-na-ba		
fly- ter-but		
cake-cup		
e-phant-le		

Activity 6 — Beat the Syllable Drum

Instructions Color each word based on its syllables following the color code provided.

Every word has a beat. Let's clap it and count it.

Color Code

Blue - one (1) syllable   **Red** - two (2) syllables
Green - three (3) syllables

hat

rocket

animal

marker

cup

bed

celery

hamburger

pilot

truck

> **Instructions** The underlined word has a missing syllable. Rewrite the sentence with the word spelled correctly.

🚀 Some syllables ran away! Can you bring them back to complete the words?

1 The <u>tele-</u> is ringing. 

---

2 We saw a <u>-bow</u> in the sky. 

---

3 My <u>-ther</u> climbed the tree. 

---

4 He used a <u>pen-</u> to draw. 

---

5 She has a new <u>-top</u>. 

Activity 8 Crack the Compound Code

Instructions Color the real compound word in each row.

Compound word means two little words = one big meaning!

1	catball	dragon	bathtub
2	moon	football	chair
3	pancake	runcup	storm
4	headlight	soapclip	nail
5	doghouse	fishstick	pearball

Activity 9 Syllable S.O.S

Instructions Each word below has three options. Color the correctly divided version.

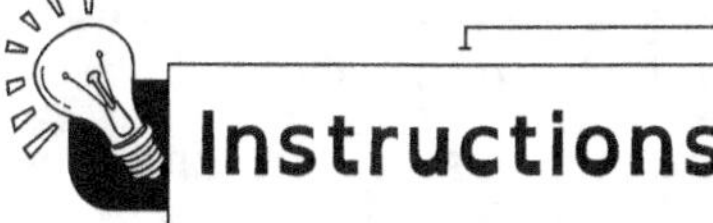

Some words got chopped in the wrong places—can you rescue them?

1	cam-e-ra	ca-me-r-a	ca-me-ra
2	sun-flo-wer	sunf-lower	su-nflower
3	ba-na-na	ban-ana	b-ana-na
4	foo-tball	footb-all	foot-ball
5	bask-et	bas-ket	ba-sket

Instructions Read the sentences. Fill in a word that rhymes with the underlined word. Then, Rewrite the sentences on the line.

Mix, match, and rhyme your way to smart syllable play!

1 She wore a red <u>hat</u>. She sat on a — — — — — —

— — — — — — — — — — — —

2 I saw a small <u>mouse</u>. It ran into the — — — — — —

— — — — — — — — — — — —

3 He flew a big <u>kite</u>. It soared out of — — — — — —

— — — — — — — — — — — —

4 They built a big <u>wall</u>. Then kicked a — — — — — —

— — — — — — — — — — — —

5 I found a green <u>bug</u>. It sat on the — — — — — —

— — — — — — — — — — — —

Unit 3 VOWEL and CONSONANT PATTERNS

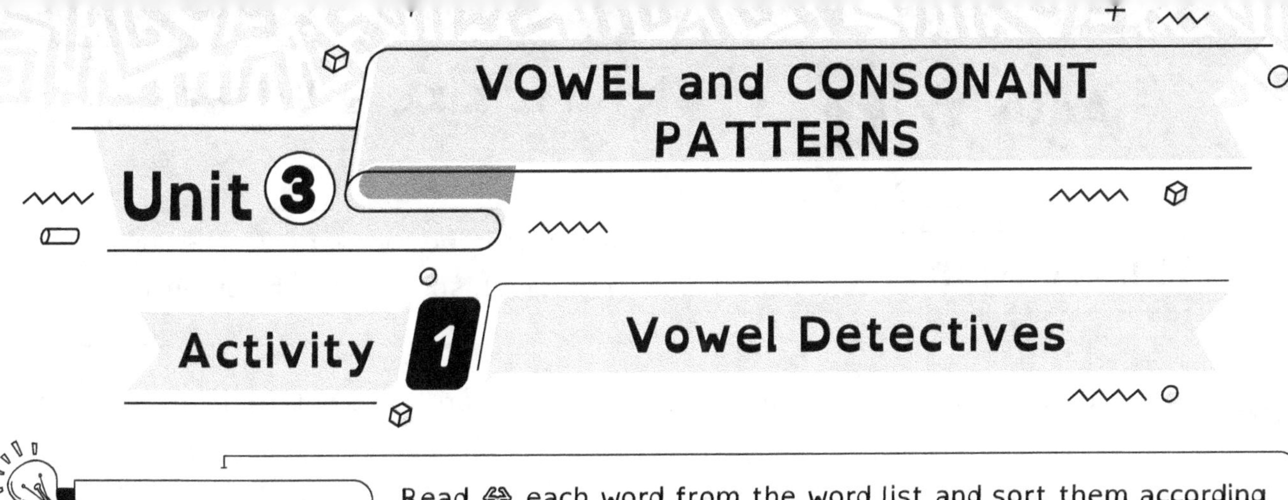

Activity 1 Vowel Detectives

Instructions Read each word from the word list and sort them according to short or long vowel sounds.

Every vowel makes a sound. Can you tell if it's short or long?

Word List

lake	mat	note	tape	bat
hop	rope	fin	pen	mule

SHORT VOWEL WORDS	LONG VOWEL WORDS

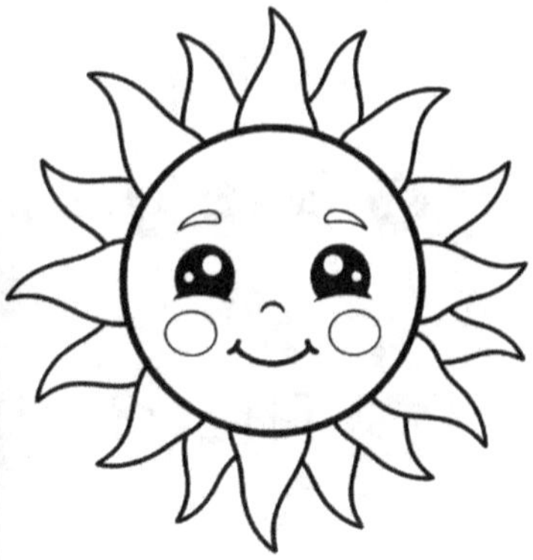

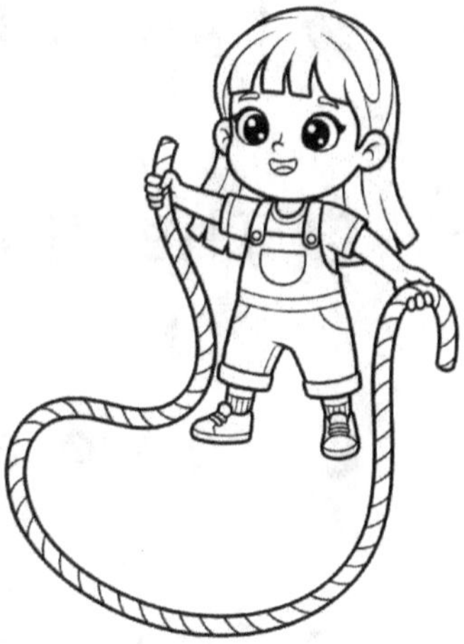

Instructions Read 👓 the sentence. Underline the word with beginning consonant blend (fr,gr, dr, sl, sn, fl) in each sentence.

Some letters team up to make a strong start, can you spot their magic blend?

1. The frog jumped into the pond.

2. I saw a tree with green leaves.

3. The drum made a loud sound.

4. We slid down the snowy hill.

5. She grabbed the red flag.

6. The snail crawled across the path.

7. I picked a pink flower for Mom.

8. The plane began to drift in the sky.

9. He wore a blue sleeve on his arm.

10. The dog chased the dragonfly by the tree.

SHHH... It's CH-Time

Instructions Copy 🖉 the sentence and circle the word/s with digraph "sh" or "ch".

🚀 Let's catch the digraph duos in action!

❶ She sat on the chair.

❷ The shark swam fast.

❸ He had cheese for lunch.

❹ I will shop for soap.

❺ We saw a shell on the beach.

Instructions Read 👓 the paragraph. Use a crayon✏️, circle ⭕ all vowel teams (like ea, ai, oa, ee, oo) and diphthongs (like oi, ow, ou, oy) following the color code provided below.

 Vowel teams are two vowels that stick together to make one sound. Diphthongs are also made of two letters, but they make a blended sound that moves your mouth while saying it.

Color Code

vowel teams - orange

diphthongs - green

Lena and I rode our boat across the blue lake to a quiet beach.

We saw a goat on the hill and heard a strange noise in

the trees. I found a smooth stone near a stream, and Lena picked up a shiny coin. A rainbow appeared in the sky, and we both shouted with joy!

Instructions Spot the spelling mistake in the sentence. Then, rewrite the sentence using the correct spelling.

 Some vowels snuck into the wrong words, can you help fix the mix-up?

1 She rode a biyk to school.

2 I will cook some rici.

3 He saw a clod sky.

4 I drew a big circlo.

5 They went to the bich to swim.

Instructions Read 👓 the paragraph below. Highlight/color ✏ every word that starts with a consonant cluster (two consonants that stick together like bl, gr, tr, sl, br, cr).

🚀 <u>Consonant clusters</u> are two or more consonants that are next to each other in a word, and you can still hear each sound.

Brenda grabbed her brush and ran to the treehouse. She wanted to plant the new flowers near the brick wall before the rain came.

A crab crawled near the gravel, and she watched it climb over a branch. Then, her brother came riding down the path on his bright blue bike. They smiled and waved as a truck passed by with a loud blast from its horn.

Instructions
Say each word aloud. Sort the words according to soft or hard "g" and "c" sounds. Write ✎ them in the correct column.

Some consonants whisper, others shout, let's sort them out!

Word List

gem goat giraffe game gift
cent cat city cereal cage

SOFT SOUND "/s/ or /j/"

LONG SOUND "/k/ or /g/"

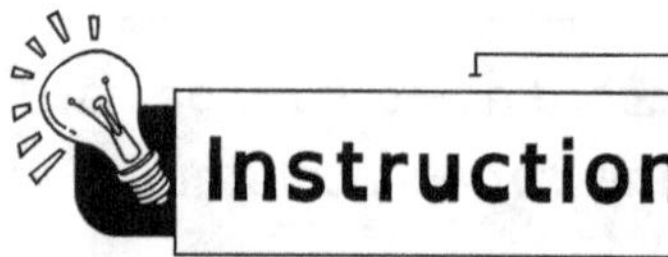

Activity 8 Meet the Magic E

Instructions Read the words below. Color the words with magic E in yellow, and the words without the magic E in orange.

Magic E is a silent letter "e" at the end of a word that makes the vowel before it say its name (the long sound).

pin

tape

cub

hug

pine

cube

tap

ripe

rip

huge

Vowel Patrol

Instructions Choose the right word from the word bank to complete the sentence. Then, rewrite the full sentence on the lines provided.

The vowels have gone missing, can you catch the right one and save the sentence?

Word Bank

cake   moon   coin   tree   pool

1 We swam in the ________________.

____

____

2 I saw a ________________ in the sky.

____

____

3 She gave me a shiny ________________.

____

____

4 He cut the ________________ into even slices.

____

____

5 We sat under the shade of a ________________.

____

____

Activity 10 Mix It, Match It, Make a Word

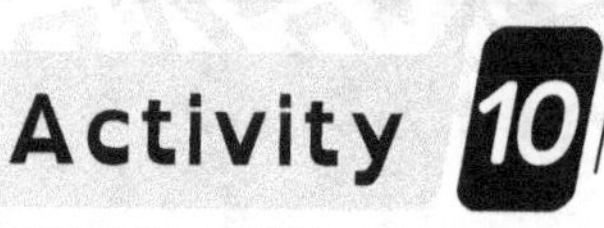

Instructions Create a rhyme chain by adding three more words that rhyme with the given word on the 1st box of each set.

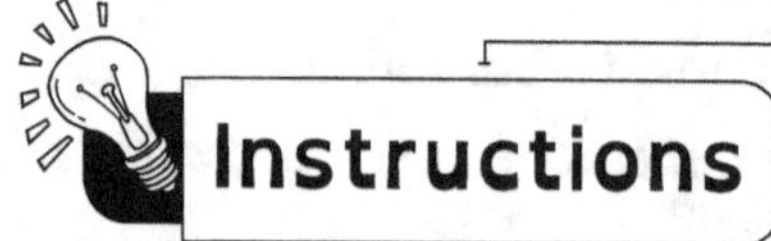

Use your vowel and consonant powers to build words that rhyme.

1. 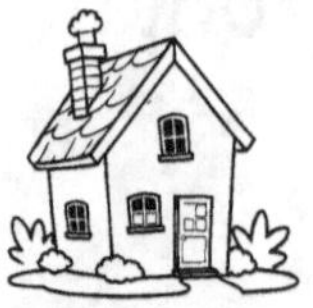
house

2. 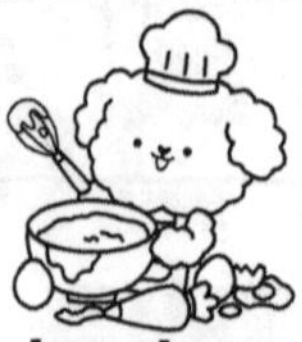
bake

3. 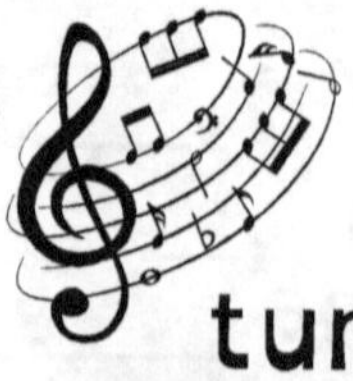
tune

4. 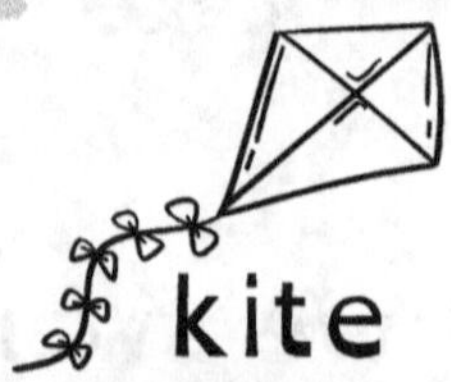
kite

Unit ④

Activity **1**   Rhyme Time Remix

Instructions Draw a line from each word to the word that rhymes with it.

Mix, match, and create rhymes that shine!

Activity  Family Word Fiesta

Instructions Write ✎ 2 more words that belong to each word family below.

<u>Word family</u> means a group of words that have the same ending sound and letters. They all rhyme and share the same spelling pattern.

1 -ell family

bell

2 -ake family

bake

3 -ore family

store

4 -eet family

feet

Instructions Finish each sentence with a rhyming word. Make it silly if you want—it's more fun!

🚀 Sharpen your ears and slice through sounds!

1. The cat wore a purple— _ _ _ _ _ _ _.

2. I saw a goat on a big— _ _ _ _ _ _.

3. The duck played drums with a— _ _ _ _ _ _ _.

4. I ate a pie and started to— _ _ _ _ _ _ _.

5. The snail told a joke to a— _ _ _ _ _ _ _.

6. I found a bear brushing his — _ _ _ _ _ _ _.

7. My dog did a dance on a— _ _ _ _ _ _ _.

8. The bug took a nap in a— _ _ _ _ _ _.

9. A mouse bounced around the— _ _ _ _ _ _ _.

10. I met a frog who sang in a— _ _ _ _ _ _.

Instructions — Pick the rhyming word from the choices to complete each sentence. Color ✏️ your answer.

Catch all the rhyming words hiding in plain sight!

1 The boy saw a goat on a ________________ .

road	boat	coat

2 The frog jumped off the log into the __________ .

pool	fog	rug

3 The cat sat on a cozy ________________ .

chair	hat	mat

4 I took a snack and had a ______________ .

nap	book	glass

5 I saw a bee land on my ______________ .

knee	bed	tree

Instructions Read  each sentence. One word doesn't rhyme like the others. Cross ✗ it out, choose the correct rhyming word from the word bank, and rewrite ✎ the sentence with the right word.

🚀 Rhymes have rules! Can you spot the word that breaks the rhyme law?

Word Bank

rug   boat   dog   rat   wig

1 A <u>frog</u> hopped onto a sleeping <u>tree</u>.

____

2 The <u>bug</u> crawled across my yellow <u>sock</u>.

____

3 I saw a <u>cat</u> sitting beside the <u>lap</u>.

____

4 The <u>pig</u> danced with a red <u>car</u> on his head.

____

5 The <u>goat</u> sailed across the sea on a big blue <u>pen</u>.

____

Instructions

Read the words in the box. Then, sort them into the correct rhyme (word) families below. Write each word in the right group.

These rhyming words all belong in a family—Help them find where they belong.

Word List

cat	goat	light	coat	night
lake	hat	bake	mat	boat

-at family

-oat family

-ight family

-ake family

Instructions   Draw a line from the beginning of each sentence to the ending that rhymes and makes the most sense.

🚀 Rhyming words make sentences sing!

1 The dog ran fast

2 I saw a red cat

3 We flew a bright kite

4 She wore a big hat

5 He jumped in the lake

6 The frog sat still

7 I played with my pup

8 The car zoomed by

9 The goat climbed high

10 A bug crawled on my rug

and gave a happy cry.

then hid inside a jug.

and finished first at last.

and saw a little snake.

and chased a little rat.

beneath the sunny sky.

until it was almost night.

and sat beside the cat.

upon the windowsill.

and filled his water cup.

Instructions   Unscramble the words to make a rhyming sentence. Use clues from the rhyming words. Write ✎ them on the line provided.

Some spellings are sneaky, let's straighten them out!

1   mat   on   sat   the   cat

____

2   boat   the   rowed   goat   the

____

3   light   the   in   kite   the   flew

____

4   log   the   on   sat   frog   the

____

5   cake   big   a   baked   Jake

____

Activity 9 — Rhyme Time Crossword

Instructions: Read each clue carefully. Use the clue to figure out the word and write it in the correct boxes on the puzzle. Make sure your spelling is correct—each word should fit perfectly!

Solve the clues, rhyme it right, and fill in the puzzle!

Word List

car	hug	bee	bell	head
kite	snake	cat	fox	train

down

1 can be found in a lake, it swims and slithers. Rhymes with "cake"

2 A furry and sneaky animal. Rhymes with "hat"

3 One of the 3 main parts of your body. Rhymes with "bed"

5 You hear it when it rings. Rhymes with "shell"

across

4 You drive it. Rhymes with star

5 It makes honey. Rhymes with "tree"

6 It flies in the sky. Rhymes with "light"

7 A tight squeeze. Rhymes with "bug"

8 A wild forest animal. Rhymes with "box"

Rhyme Like a Poet

Instructions Use two rhyming word pairs to write a 4-line poem. It can be silly, sweet, or about something you love! Choose your words pairs from the list below.

 Ready to be a rhyme-writing superstar?

Word Pairs List

sky / fly cake / lake	bee/ tree night / light	goat / boat cat / rat

Unit 5 GRAPHEMES AND PHONEMES

Activity 1 Sound it Out

Instructions In each row, color ✏ the one word that matches the phoneme shown.

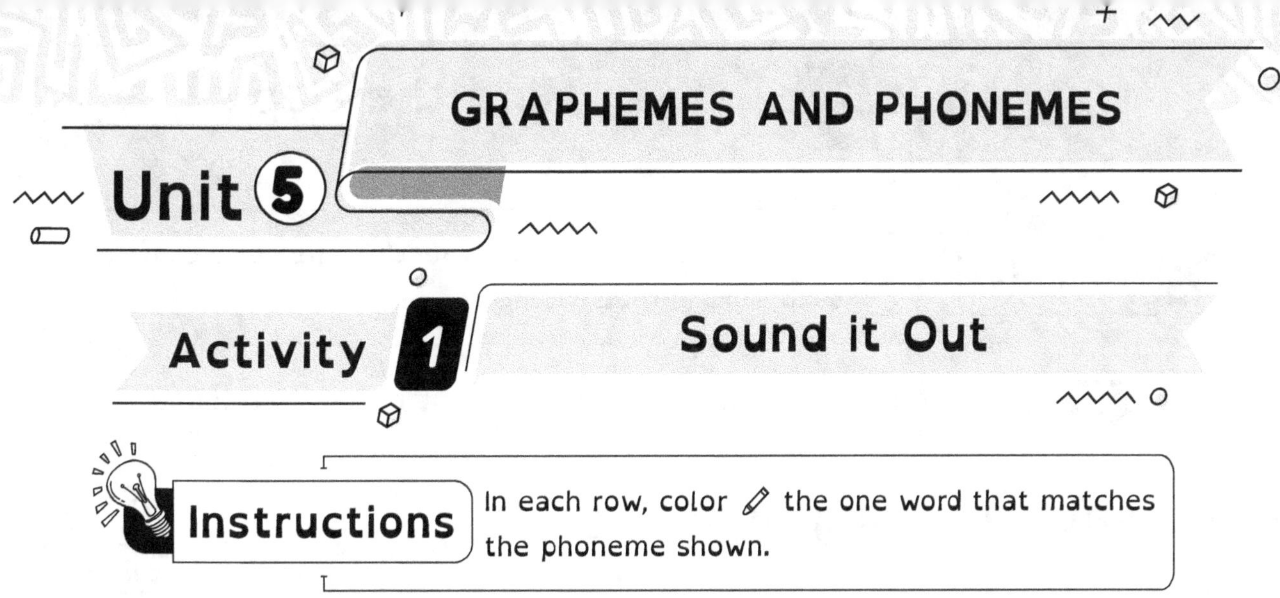

A phoneme is a sound. A grapheme is the letter or letters that make that sound.

/sh/	cat	ship	log
/ch/	fan	pet	chat
/th/	bell	bath	duck
/ow/	now	net	feet

Instructions Fill in the blank with the correct grapheme to complete each word in the sentence.

A <u>grapheme</u> is the letter or letters that make that sound.

1. We sat on a long ben______.

2. She sat in the comfy ______air.

3. The baby saw a pink dol______in.

4. Mom bought a new cell______one.

5. The ______ark swam fast in the sea.

6. The ______ickens ran around the farm.

7. He brushed his tee______ every night.

8. The ______eels of the bike were rusty.

9. I heard a loud ______out from the crowd.

10. Dad built a new ______elves for my sister.

Read 👓 the paragraph. Circle ⭕ all the words that contain the /f/ sound (spelled as f or ph).

🚀 Some sounds wear disguises!

Felix found a funny photo on his phone. The photo showed a fish, a fan, and an elephant in a bath! He laughed and sent the photo to his friend Phil.Phil fell off the sofa when he saw the photo. Then they drew a giraffe surfing with a dolphin and a floppy hat. Felix's father printed the photo and pinned it on the fridge. They called it "The Fantastic Photo of the Year!"

Activity 4 — Great Grapheme Fix-Up

Instructions Fill in the missing grapheme to complete each word in the sentence. Then, copy ✍ the sentence.

🚀 Some letters team up to make one sound!

1 The _____air was broken, so I sat on the floor.

2 I heard a loud _____ump from the hallway.

3 We read a story about a dol_____in.

4 Please brush your tee_____ before bed.

5 _____at is your name?

Oops! Fix That Sound

Instructions The sentences below have words with incorrect graphemes. Rewrite ✎ the sentences with correct spelling.

🚀 Some letters are quiet, but they still count!

1 I used my <u>fone</u> to call mom.

2 The <u>whuorlwend</u> blew the leaves away.

3 We saw a <u>jorilla</u> at the zoo.

4 The <u>cheep</u> ran through the grass.

5 My brother lost his <u>tumb</u> bandage.

Unscramble the letters to form a word. Each word includes a focus grapheme! Write it on the blank next to it, then use the word in a sentence.

The jungle of letters is full of scrambled words waiting to be untangled!

1 tnhor

2 fsih

3 rweit

4 kcenihc

5 eeesch

Instructions   Read 👓 the paragraph carefully. <u>Underline</u> all the words that include the grapheme "igh" (like in light or bright).

🚀 Certain letters team up to make long sounds.

It was a bright night, and the sky was full of stars. The moon gave off a soft light that made the trees shine. I saw a kite flying high over the hill, dancing in the sky. Right next to me, an owl took flight and flapped its wings. Then,

a fox ran right past me with a flashlight in its mouth! I stood still with fright, but it dashed out of sight. My friend gave me a slight nudge and said, "That was a wild night!"

Instructions Fix the grapheme mistake in each sentence and rewrite the sentence using the correctly spelled grapheme on the line provided.

Graphemes are groups of letters that make one sound.

1 I read a boock in bed.

____

2 We rode a trane to the zoo.

____

3 A huge starm hit the town last night.

____

4 She picked a flouer for her mom.

____

5 The sun will shine after the rayne.

____

Activity 9 — Grapheme Puzzle Lab

Instructions Use the grapheme in each box to build a real word. Then, write ✎ the word and draw ✏ a picture of it!

🚀 It's time to solve word puzzles using sound pieces!

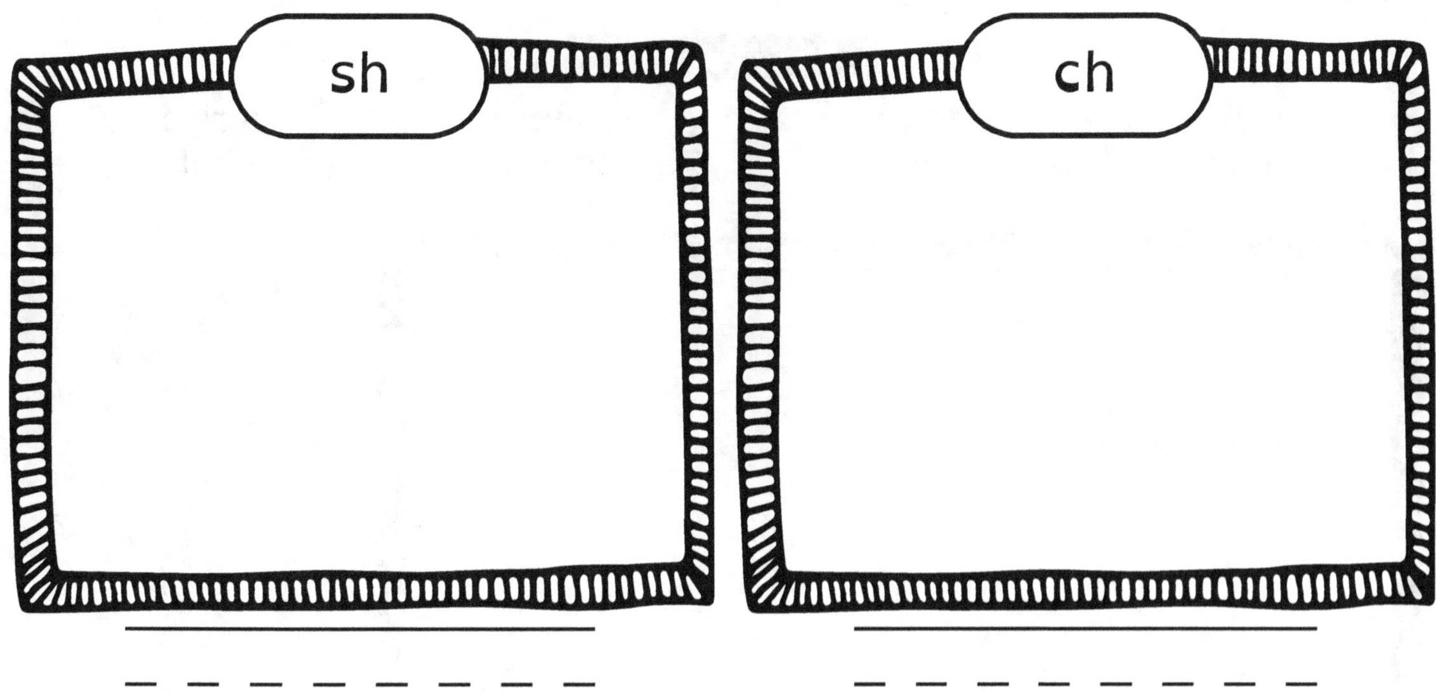

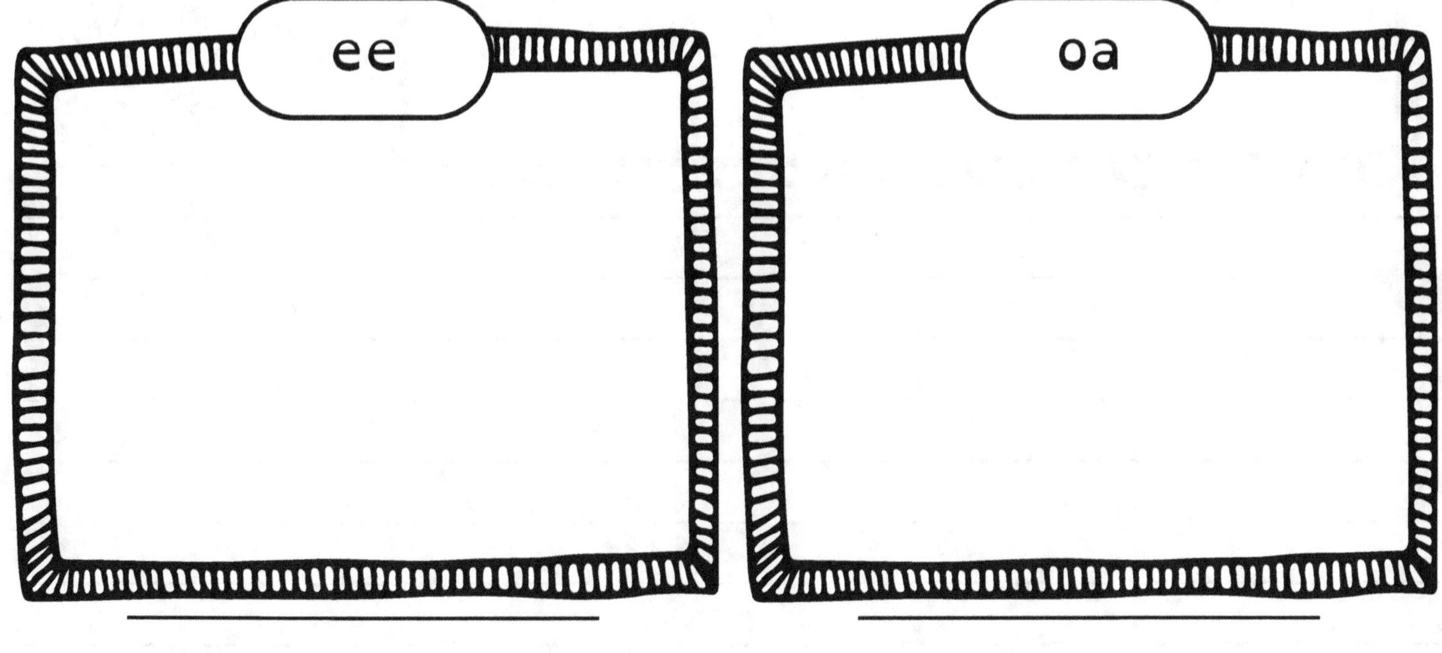

Great Grapheme Tale

Instructions Write ✏ your own short story (4–6 sentences). Use at least 3 words from the grapheme list below. <u>Underline</u> the grapheme word in each sentence. Draw ✏ a scene from your story.

🚀 A <u>grapheme</u> is a group of letters that make a sound, like sh in "sheep" or ph in "phone."

Word Pairs List

ship	think	sheep	write
chair	thumb	phone	whale

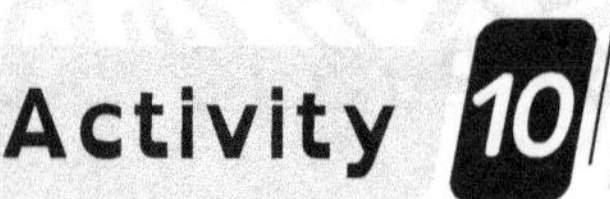

Unit 6

Activity 1 — Prefix Power

Instructions Add the correct prefix to each root word to create a new word. Use the new word in a sentence!

A <u>prefix</u> is a word part that comes at the beginning of a word and changes its meaning.

1 write (un, re, pre) – — — — — — — — —

2 lock (dis, pre, un) – — — — — — — —

3 behave (pre, dis, mis) — — — — — — — — —

4 agree (dis, re, un) – — — — — — — —

Activity **2** — Super Suffix Builders

Instructions Add a suffix to the word in parentheses then rewrite the sentence using the new word.

Suffixes are word endings that add power, personality, or purpose to base words.

1 Be (care) that pot is hot!

2 He is (run) around the playground.

3 The (teach) explained the lesson

4 I (quick) packed my bag.

5 The (hope) girl smiled at her friend.

Root Word Rescue

Instructions Separate each word into its prefix, root, and suffix (if any) by completing the chart below.

Every word has a root—like a seed that gives it meaning!

WORD	PREFIX	ROOT WORD	SUFFIX
1 redo			
2 hopeful			
3 disrespectful			
4 unkind			
5 unfriendly			
6 replay			
7 preheat			
8 disagree			

Instructions — Use the root word and clue in parentheses to build the correct word with a prefix or suffix.

Prefixes and suffixes are like LEGO pieces for words. Stick them on to change meaning!

1 He was very _ _ _ _ _ _ _ _ (care + ful).

2 I had to _ _ _ _ _ _ _ _ (write + again) my paper.

3 She moved very _ _ _ _ _ _ _ _ (quick + ly).

4 They were _ _ _ _ _ _ _ _ (hope + less).

5 We saw ten _ _ _ _ _ _ _ _ _ (run + ers) in the race.

6 She is a _ _ _ _ _ _ _ _ (teach + er) at my school.

7 I will _ _ _ _ _ _ _ _ (do + again) my homework.

8 She was _ _ _ _ _ _ _ _ _ (help + ful) with the chores.

Instructions

Complete the sentence by writing ✎ the opposite word (antonym) of the word enclosed in parenthesis. Then circle ○ the prefix.

🚀 Common <u>prefixes that show opposites</u> are like un-, dis-, in-, and im-.

1 She felt (happy) — — — — — — — — when her team lost.

2 That tiny bug was almost (visible) — — — — — — — — —.

3 The rules of the game felt (fair) — — — — — — — — —.

4 You should not (obey) — — — — — — — — — your parents.

5 That box is (possible) — — — — — — — — — to lift.

6 My shirt is (clean) — — — — — — — — — from playing.

7 She is feeling (lucky) — — — — — — — — — today.

8 I (agree) — — — — — — — — — with your idea.

Instructions

Use a word from the Root Word Bank to complete each sentence.

A <u>root word</u> is the basic part of a word. It carries the main meaning.

Root Word Bank

write	swim	jump	read	play
draw	cook	build	paint	help

1 I love to — — — — — — — — with my friends at recess.

2 She asked her friend to — — — — — — — — her carry books.

3 We used bright colors to — — — — — — — the walls.

4 Dad will — — — — — — a new birdhouse for the backyard.

5 I will — — — — — — — — a chapter before bed.

6 We like to — — — — — — — — in the pool on hot days.

7 I want to — — — — — — — — a card to my grandma.

Affix Explorer

Instructions Sort the words into the correct group based on whether they have prefixes, suffixes, or both.

 Words can wear special costumes called <u>prefixes (at the beginning)</u> and <u>suffixes (at the end).</u>

Word List

unreadable   retell   dislike   preheat
kindness   painter   helpful   smiling

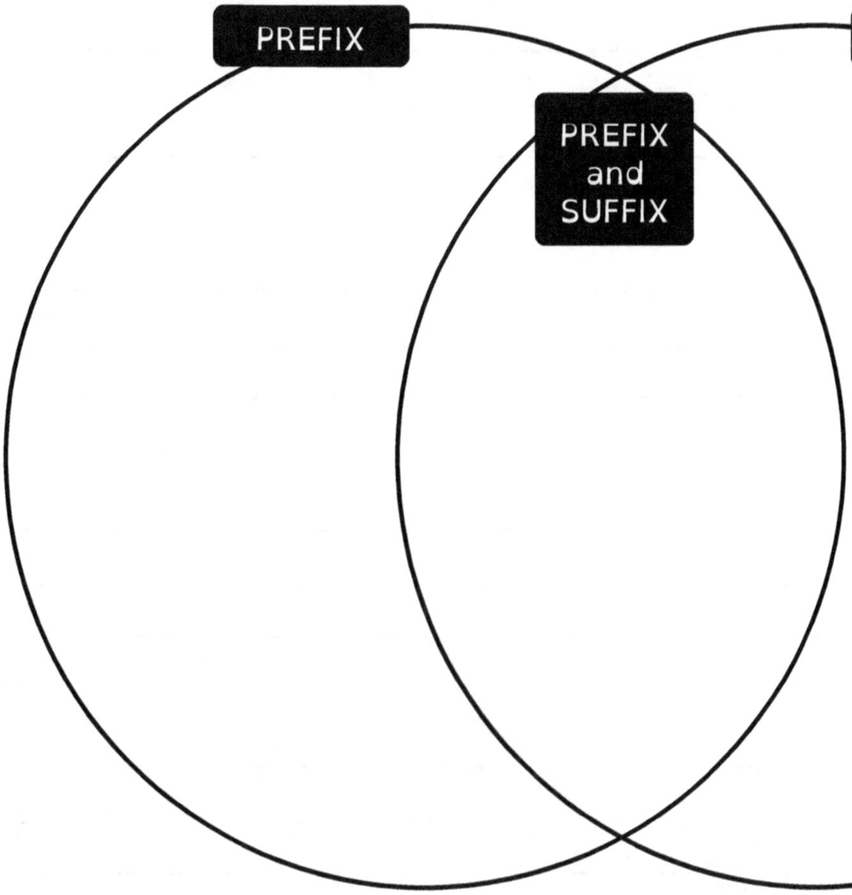

PREFIX

SUFFIX

PREFIX and SUFFIX

Instructions Use the word in a sentence.

Prefixes and suffixes change the meaning of a word—but when we use them in sentences, they really come to life!

❶ helpful

____

- - - - - - - - - - - - - - - - - -

❷ unfair

____

- - - - - - - - - - - - - - - - - -

❸ retell

____

- - - - - - - - - - - - - - - - - -

❹ careless

____

- - - - - - - - - - - - - - - - - -

❺ rewrite

____

- - - - - - - - - - - - - - - - - -

Instructions   Solve the riddle by thinking about the word parts.

<u>Morphology</u> means studying the parts of words to understand what they mean.

1 I start with "re-" and I mean to do something again.

What word am I?— — — — — — — — — — — —

2 I start with "un-" and mean you are not kind.

What word am I?— — — — — — — — — — — —

3 I start with "re-" and I mean to look again.

What word am I?— — — — — — — — — — — —

4 I end in "-er" and I mean someone who teaches.

What word am I?— — — — — — — — — — — —

5 I start with "mis-" and I mean to behave badly.

What word am I?— — — — — — — — — — — —

Instructions — Combine one prefix, one root, and one suffix to make a real word. Then, use the word in a sentence.

Build brand-new words like a word wizard! Just stack a prefix in the front, a root word in the middle, and a suffix at the end!

PREFIX	ROOT WORD	SUFFIX	NEW WORD
un-	kind	-ness	
re-	play	-ing	
dis-	like	----	
----	help	-ful	

Unit 7

Activity 1 — Fill It In, Fix It Up

Instructions Use the words from the word bank to fill in each blank so the sentence makes sense.

Some sentences are missing important words—like cookies missing chocolate chips!

Word Bank

ball　　dog　　sleepy　　run　　rabbit

1. The — — — — — — — — is barking loudly.

2. She likes to — — — — — — — — —in the yard.

3. He threw the — — — — — — — — to his friend.

4. The — — — — — — — —kitten sat on the windowsill.

5. This — — — — — — — — is soft and furry.

Instructions   Unscramble the sentence fragments to form a complete sentence. Start each sentence with a capital letter and end with the correct punctuation.

 Sentences are like puzzles, they need the right pieces in the right order!

1 ball / the / kicked / he

2 cat / the / under / slept / table / the

3 I / sandwich / my / ate / lunch / for

4 sang / bird / the / tree / the / in

5 ran / quickly / she / playground / the / to

Activity **3** — "Oops! Fix That Sentence!

Instructions — Each sentence or story has a mistake. Find the error, fix it, and rewrite ✏ the sentence the right way. Let's turn broken sentences into perfect ones!

Sometimes sentences get a little messy, but that's okay! We're going to spot what's wrong, clean it up, and make our writing shine like a star!

1 she goed to the store.

2 we playd at the park.

3 my cat is name tigger.

4 i am runned fast.

5 he eat all the cookie?

Instructions Use the words from each word bank to write ✏ a clear and complete sentence.

🚀 A complete sentence needs a who or what, an action, and a full idea. Don't forget your capital letter and punctuation!

① **WORD BANK** bird, flies, sky

② **WORD BANK** boy, kicks, ball

③ **WORD BANK** mom, bakes, cake

④ **WORD BANK** fish, swims, water

⑤ **WORD BANK** dog, runs, park

Picture This

Instructions — Look at each picture and write one full sentence to describe what you see.

A picture is worth a thousand words, so let's start with one perfect sentence!

Activity **6** — **Word Detectives!**

Instructions Read each sentence. With the use of crayon, highlight the <u>noun in blue</u>, <u>verb in green</u> and the <u>adjective in red</u>.

A <u>noun</u> names a person, place, or thing. A <u>verb</u> shows action. An <u>adjective</u> describes a noun.

1. The big dog barked loudly.

2. She wore a pretty dress.

3. The fast car zoomed away.

4. My brother kicked the ball.

5. A tall giraffe walked slowly.

6. A small bird chirped in the tree.

7. The cold juice spilled on the floor.

8. The shiny apple rolled off the table.

9. The loud thunder shook the windows.

10. The sleepy cat stretched on the couch.

Instructions | Look closely at each sentence. It's missing punctuation! Add a period (.), question mark (?), exclamation point (!) or comma (,) to make it correct. Then rewrite ✎ the sentence on the line below.

🚀 Every sentence needs the right punctuation to be complete!

❶ Where did you put my backpack

____

- -

____

❷ I love apples bananas and grapes

____

- -

____

❸ My dog is very funny

____

- -

____

❹ Can we play outside now

____

- -

____

❺ Wow that was amazing

____

- -

____

Instructions Use each word prompt to write 🖊 a complete sentence.

With just a word, your imagination can take off!

1 rainy day

2 school bus

3 snowman

4 library

5 handwritten letters

Instructions Read 👓 each sentence. Rewrite ✎ the sentence by changing the words, adding new details, or making it longer. You may add a color word, a word to tell how, or you may use a stronger verb to improve it!

🚀 Plain sentences? Not anymore!

1 The cat sleeps.

2 They eat lunch.

3 The car goes fast.

4 I saw a bird.

5 The boy is happy.

Activity 10 — From Bits to Big Ideas

Instructions

Put the 4 sentence fragments in the correct order to build a paragraph. Write ✏ them in the right order with proper punctuation and draw ✏ a scene from the paragraph in the box.

Sentences are like puzzle pieces, when you put them in the right order, they make an awesome paragraph!

Sentence Fragments

We saw lions, monkeys, and elephants.

It was my first trip to the zoo.

I can't wait to go back!

I loved watching the monkeys swing on the ropes.

Sentence Building   Unit 7

CONTEXT CLUES AND WORD USAGE

Unit 8

Activity 1 — Clue Crew

Instructions Read 👓 the paragraph and write ✍ the meaning of the <u>underlined words</u> using clues from the story.

🚀 Use clues in the sentence to figure out the right word that fits best.

I was <u>shivering</u> as I walked

into the cold room.

I grabbed a <u>blanket</u> and sat near the heater.

My hands were <u>numb</u>,

and my teeth were <u>chattering</u>.

Slowly, I started to feel warm again.

1 shivering — — — — — — — — — — — — — — — — — —

2 blanket — — — — — — — — — — — — — — — — — —

3 numb — — — — — — — — — — — — — — — — — —

4 chattering — — — — — — — — — — — — — — — — — —

Instructions Read each sentence. Circle ○ the word that means the same as the <u>underlined</u> word.

A <u>synonym</u> is a word that means the same or almost the same as another word.

1 The <u>small</u> dog chased a tiny ball.

2 The fast train passed the <u>quick</u> car.

3 She was glad to see her <u>happy</u> friend.

4 We had a clean room and a <u>neat</u> table.

5 It was a <u>cold</u> night with a chilly breeze.

6 He was angry after the <u>mad</u> game ended.

7 She felt <u>sad</u> when her unhappy pet ran away.

8 The <u>big</u> elephant walked beside a large truck.

9 I was too tired to play, so I took a <u>sleepy</u> nap.

10 He was very <u>smart</u> and knew the correct clever answer.

Instructions Rewrite ✍ the sentences with the antonym of the <u>underlined word</u> to change their meaning!

🚀 An <u>antonym</u> is a word that means the opposite of another word.

1 The water is <u>cold</u>.

2 She is a <u>quiet</u> student.

3 My dog is <u>small</u>.

4 We walked on a <u>clean</u> floor.

5 This puzzle is <u>easy</u>.

Instructions Some words have more than one meaning. Read 👓 each sentence carefully and circle ◯ the word that can have two meanings.

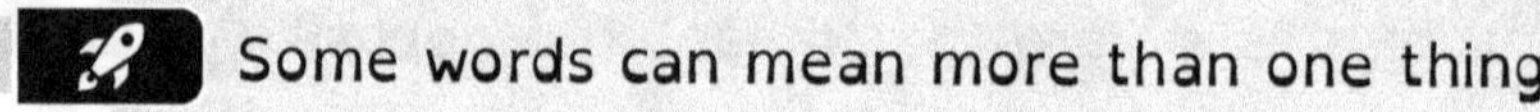

1 The bat flew out of the dark cave.
He swung the bat and hit a home run.

2 I need to go to the bank to get money.
We sat by the bank of the river.

3 The duck saw a tear fall from her eye.
Be careful not to tear the paper.

4 I saw a bark on the tree trunk.
My dog began to bark at the mailman.

5 She wore a ring on her finger.
I heard the phone ring in the kitchen.

6 The rock was smooth and round.
We will rock the baby to sleep.

7 He used a pen to write a story.
The goat stayed in the pen near the barn.

8 I'll watch a movie tonight.
Please give me your watch so I can check the time.

Activity 5 — Pick the Right Clue

Instructions Draw a line to match the context phrase with its meaning.

Use the clues in each sentence to find the word that makes sense!

PHRASE	MEANING
1 "He raced down the track."	started laughing suddenly
2 "She burst into laughter."	it might rain soon
3 "He gave a puzzled look."	looked confused
4 "The sky turned gray and cloudy."	they were very happy and loud
5 "They cheered with excitement."	ran quickly

Instructions Fill in each blank using the words from the word bank.

Word Bank

ants   basket   grass   juice   blanket

"Picnic Story Zone"

We went on a picnic in the park.

We laid out our _______________ and sat on

the soft _______________.

Mom brought a big _______________ full of food.

I drank orange _______________ .

Then, we saw the _______________ crawling

toward our sandwiches!

Instructions Read each sentence. Underline the word that is used incorrectly.

Some words sound alike but are used differently. These are called <u>homophones</u> (like "there" and "their") different things!

1. I no how to ride a bike.

2. The dog wagged it's tail.

3. I ate a hole apple in one bite.

4. She read a story out loud to her sun.

5. Their going to the movie after lunch.

6. He through the ball through the window.

7. I went to the store to by milk and bread.

8. The hare brushed his hare before bedtime.

9. Please take a break and eat you're snack.

10. The night rode his horse through the night.

Instructions Read 👀 each riddle and color ✏️ the word that correctly answers it.

🚀 Use the hints in each riddle to figure out the mystery word!

1 I have hands but no arms. I tell you the time.

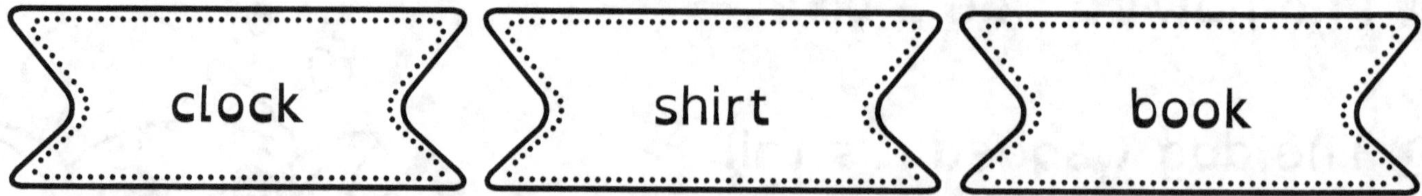

2 I can run, but I never walk. I have a bed, but I never sleep.

3 I go up but never come down.

4 I'm hot and bright, and help you see during the day.

5 I dry you off when you're wet.

Activity 9 — Same Word, New World

Instructions — Words can have more than one meaning! Write ✍ two different sentences using the same word that show different meanings.

🚀 Some words wear different hats! One word can mean many things depending on where and how it's used.

❶ bat

Sentence 1

Sentence 2

❷ wave

Sentence 1

Sentence 2

❸ watch

Sentence 1

Sentence 2

❹ spring

Sentence 1

Sentence 2

Activity 10 — Double Duty Words

Instructions Some words can mean different things in different places. Use the clues in the story to figure out the correct meaning and fill in the blanks.

Some words are extra busy—they can mean more than one thing!

Word Bank

trunk   wave   nail

At the zoo, we saw an elephant move its big __________ __ __ __ __ __ __ __ __ __.

Later, I opened the car's __ __ __ __ __ __ __ __ to get my backpack.

On the beach, we saw the ocean's huge __________ __ __ __ __ __ __ __ __ __ crashing on the sand.

Then, my friend gave me a big __________ __ __ __ __ __ __ __ __ from far away!

We hung up the sign with a __ __ __ __ __ __ __ __ __,

but then I broke one __ __ __ __ __ __ __ __ while climbing the fence!

Unit 9

Activity 1 — Sentence Sparkers

Instructions — Look at each picture. Write 🖊 a complete sentence about it.

🚀 Turn tiny clues into terrific sentences!

Paragraph Puzzle

Instructions Number the sentences (1, 2, 3, 4) in the correct order. Then, write ✎ them in sequential order to form a paragraph.

🚀 A good paragraph is like a puzzle—all the sentences fit together!

○ The lights went dark, and everyone cheered.

○ I went to the fair with my family.

○ We rode the Ferris wheel and ate popcorn.

○ At night, there was a big fireworks show.

Scramble to Story

Instructions Read 👓 each sentence carefully. Number (1, 2, 3, 4) the sentences to show the right order of the story. Rewrite ✐ 🖌 the story in the correct order using clue words like First, Then, Next, and Finally to make it flow smoothly.

🚀 Stories love good order!

Scrambled Sentences

☐ The sun was shining, so we packed a basket.

☐ We spread out a blanket under the big oak tree.

☐ We ate sandwiches and drank lemonade.

☐ After lunch, we played soccer in the park.

Instructions Fill in the missing adjectives to complete the story. Use fun, describing words!

An <u>adjective</u> is a word that describes a noun (a person, place, thing, or animal). It tells what kind, how many, or which one.

Today, I went to the ___________ beach. The ___________ waves splashed at my feet. I built a ___________ sandcastle. Later, I will eat a ___________ ice cream and watch the ___________ sunset. A ___________ crab crawled near my towel. The breeze was ___________ and made the palm trees sway. Before I left, I took a ___________ photo to remember the day.

Instructions — Read the story carefully. Use the clues to fill in the blanks with words from the word bank. Then, <u>underline</u> the clues that helped you decide!

Every word you choose helps the story come alive! So, choose the right words.

Word Bank

balloons   cake   presents   party   music

Today was my birthday, and it was the best day ever! I had a big _______ with all my friends. We played _______ and danced around the room. After that, we shared a giant chocolate _____ and laughed together. I opened all my colorful ________ and found amazing toys inside! Bright _______ floated up to the ceiling and made the room look magical.

Instructions — Read 👓 the story carefully. With the use of your crayons ✏️, color the adjectives (describing nouns) red and the adverbs (describing verbs) green.

🚀 <u>Adjectives</u> make nouns more interesting! <u>Adverbs</u> give more details about actions!

The tiny kitten jumped happily onto the soft pillow. It batted the shiny ball quickly across the smooth floor. Everyone clapped loudly when the kitten made a flip!

Then, the kitten chased a striped feather across the wooden room. It landed swiftly on a fluffy rug and yawned sleepily.

Later, the curious kitten peeked into a tall basket and batted a crinkly wrapper. The excited children laughed cheerfully as the kitten rolled gently on the floor.

Suddenly, it spotted a colorful butterfly by the open window and pounced gracefully. The bright sunlight warmed its fuzzy fur as it stretched slowly.

After all the fun, the tired kitten curled up beside a warm blanket and fell asleep peacefully.
What a silly, happy day with the adorable kitten!

Activity 7 — Word Bank Wonders

Instructions Complete the story by adding at least 3-4 sentences using ALL the words in the word bank.

Use the magic of words to build your own exciting story!

Word Bank

treasure	jungle	escape	brave

Maya found an old map hidden inside a dusty book. It showed a secret path leading to an island...

Instructions — Circle ◯ all the grammar, capitalization and spelling mistakes in the silly fairy tale below. Then, rewrite ✍ the story correctly on the lines.

Find the mistakes and turn them into fantastic, polished tales.

once upon a time, a littel gurl and her frend goed to the magic park. they climed a tree that taked them to the cloudz. they eated rainbow ice creem and playd with flying unicorns. it was the funnest day ever!

Activity 9   Story Shuffle

Instructions Read the story pieces below. Then, write them in the correct order on the lines. Use your own transition words (like First, Then, Next, Finally) to help the story flow smoothly!

Transition words are words that help connect ideas in a sentence or story. They show what happens first, next, after, or last, so the story makes sense and flows smoothly.

STORY PIECES

- Sam packed his backpack for school.
- Sam brushed his teeth and washed his face.
- Sam waved goodbye and walked to the bus stop.
- Sam got dressed and ate breakfast.
- Sam woke up when his alarm rang.

Instructions Use the sentence fragments to create your own story by putting the ideas in order and adding extra details to make it exciting! Use all the fragments to complete your story.

The story pieces are scattered! Put them together into an awesome adventure.

SENTENCE FRAGMENTS

- The pirate found a dusty old map.
- A storm tossed the ship at sea.
- They dug under the biggest tree on the island.
- The crew danced around the treasure chest!

Unit 10

Activity 1 — Rhyme Time Rescue

Instructions Read 👓 the passage. Complete the story by filling in the missing rhyming words.

🚀 Turn reading into a rhyming adventure!

The bird can sing,

It flaps its __________.

It flies so high,

Up in the __________!

The cat takes a nap,

Curled in a __________.

It dreams of fish,

And makes a __________.

> **Instructions**   Read the story. Circle ○ the graphemes "sh," "ch," "th," and "ph."

A <u>grapheme</u> is the letter or letters that make that sound.

Charlie dashed to the shop with his brother to find something special.

They picked out a shiny photo frame and a fresh fish for dinner.

At the counter, they saw thick chocolate bars and creamy milkshakes.

They chose strawberry shakes to share and paid with a photograph-themed gift card.

After shopping, they chatted, laughed, and skipped down the path.

Then, they sat on a bench near the fountain and sipped their shakes.

A nearby cat chased a butterfly, making them giggle even more.

It was truly the best shopping trip they had ever shared!

Grapheme Gap Adventure

Instructions Choose the correct grapheme (sh, ch, th, ph) to complete each word in the story.

Be Grapheme Hero by filling in the graphemes to complete the story!

One sunny day, I went to the fi___ pond.

A big ___air was set up under a ___ady tree.

I saw a little dol___in jumping near the rocks!

My bro___er and I ran to the ___op to buy

a yummy ice cream. We shared a ___ocolate

cone and sat on the green grass. A butterfly

flew by and landed on my ___oulder!

We even took a silly ___oto to

remember the day.

What a fun adventure we had!

Instructions Read each sentence. Cross out ✗ the wrong word and rewrite the sentence using the corrected word.

1 She was unhelped when setting the table.

2 My backpack was heavly with books.

3 The dog was playness in the park.

4 He is dishappy with his test score.

5 We misbuild our project yesterday.

Activity 5 — Silly Syllable Fix-Up

Instructions: Fill in the blanks with the appropriate syllables by choosing and coloring ✏ your answer on the options provided.

1 The dog began to ____low us through the park.

2 I saw a bright ____terfly land on a flower.

3 Dad ____lished the car until it was shiny.

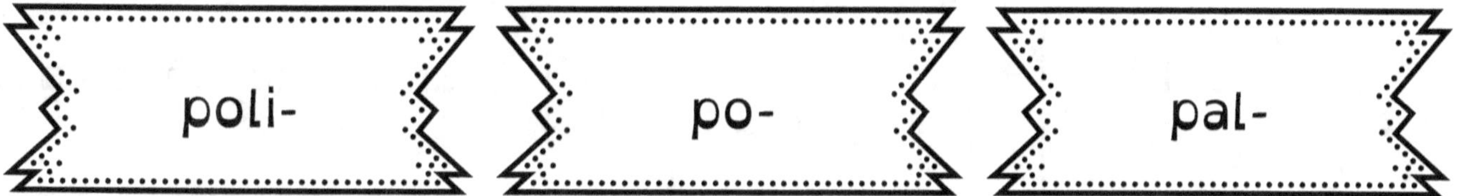

4 We walked to the ____ket to buy fresh fruit.

5 She put the ____wers into a big vase.

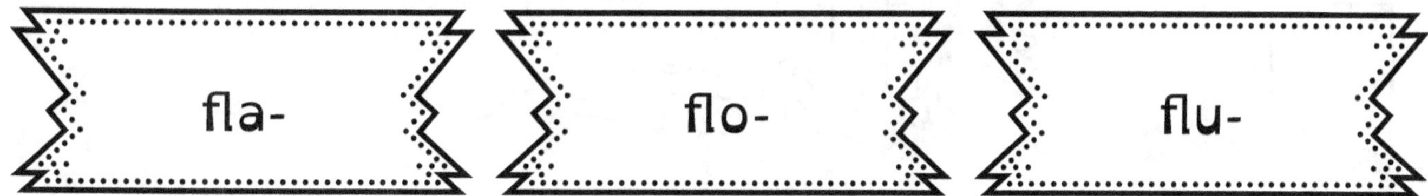

Instructions Read 👓 the clues. Use the hints to fill in the crossword puzzle.

🚀 Every word you figure out will unlock part of the big picture.

Word Bank

shoes   bus   day   library   dog   apple

down

1 A place where you borrow books.

2 Something you wear on your feet

5 an animal that barks.

across

3 A yellow thing you ride to school.

4 A fruit that is red or green.

5 The opposite of night.

Instructions   Pick two pairs of rhyming words. Use them to write ✎ your own fun four-line poem. Make it silly, sweet, or surprising! Then, draw ✏ a picture of your poem in the box.

🚀   A <u>rhyme</u> is when two or more words sound the same at the end.

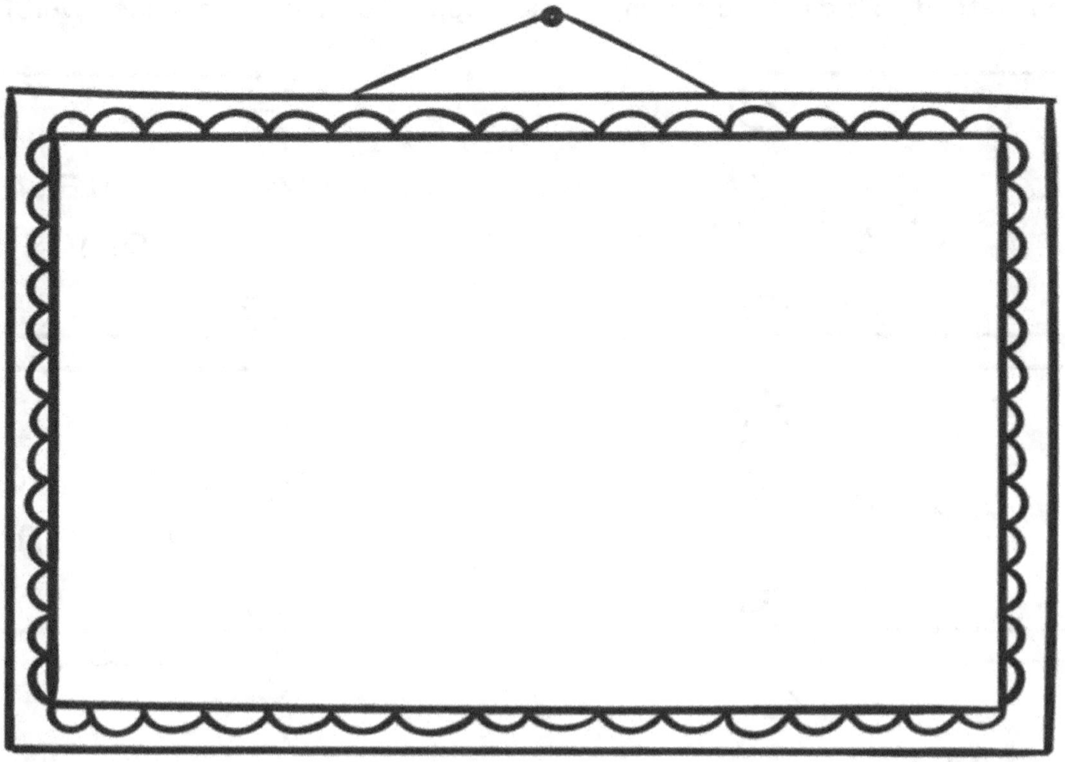

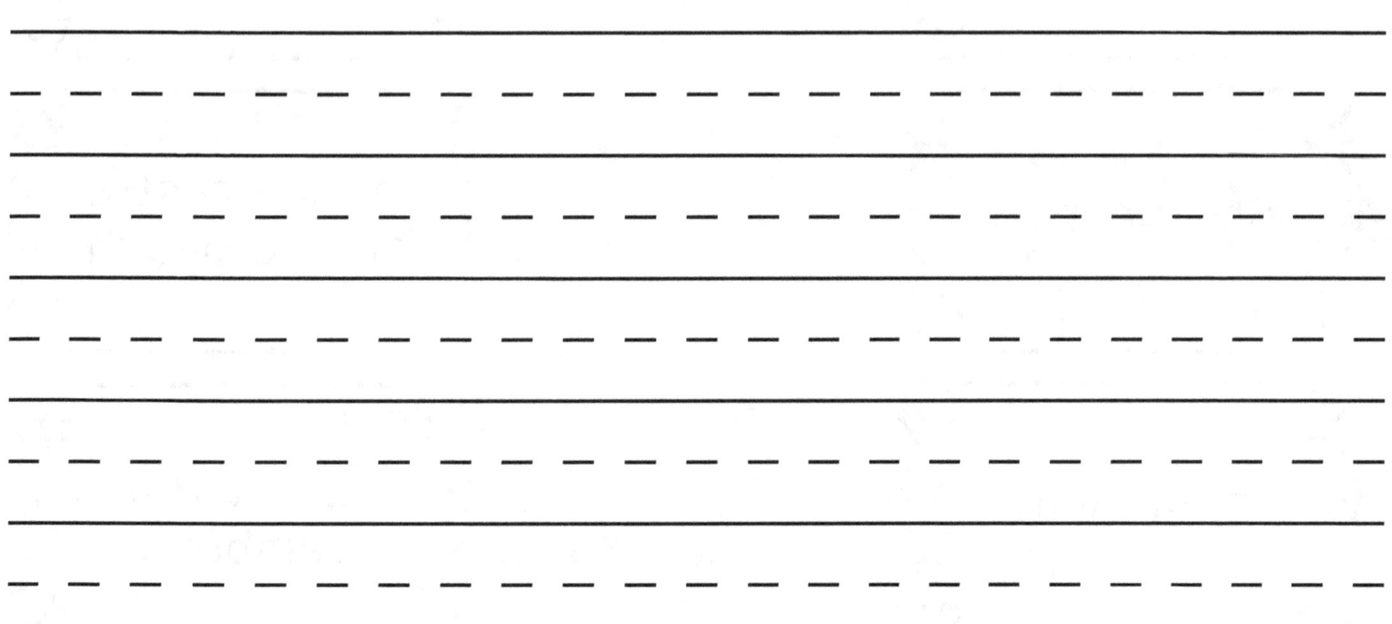

Instructions   Draw a line to connect the sentence beginning on the left with the correct ending on the right.

A <u>sentence fragment</u> is a group of words that looks like a sentence but doesn't tell a complete idea. It might be missing a who (subject) or a what happened (verb).

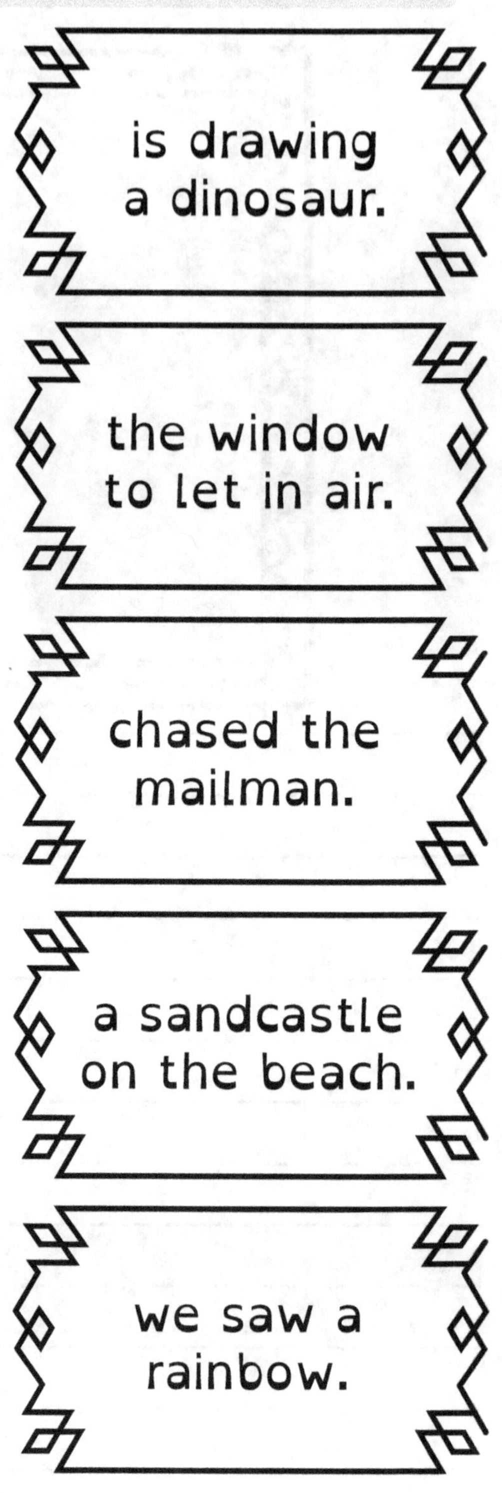

Activity 9 — Grapheme Adventures

Instructions Choose a beginning, middle, and end from the list. Then write ✎ a silly story using all three parts! Your story should be 4–6 sentences long. Circle ○ the graphemes (sh, ch, th, ph) in your story!

 Say it. Hear it. Choose the word that sounds just right!

BEGINNINGS
- A chick danced on the playground.
- A thick cloud floated across the sky.

MIDDLES
- The water started to sparkle.
- The chair flew away!

ENDINGS
- Everyone cheered and clapped.
- It rained chocolate chips!

Crack the Word Code

Instructions Use the clues below to fill in the crossword. Each word connects to your phonics, rhyming, or vocabulary lessons.

Word Bank

- cake
- hot
- chair
- kite
- wave
- chicken
- shoes
- frog

down

1 begins with a grapheme "ch" and has 2 syllables, something you can eat

3 rhymes with site and flies in the sky

5 rhymes with lake

across

2 the opposite of cold

4 something you sit on

6 a sound you hear on the beach

7 start with "sh" , and you wear them on your feet

8 a type of animal that jumps

Instructions Read the story below. Circle at least 8 mistakes. Then, rewrite the story correctly on the lines.

once upon a time, a boy named leo goed camping with his dad. their was a big, blue tent. Leo was so excited he runned to the lake? He seed a frog on a log and a fish with shiny skales. For dinner, they eated hot dogs over the fire. the stars were so bright. It was the funnest adventure ever. Leo feeled very happy and tired.

Activity Now, write the corrected story here:

____
- -
____
- -
____
- -
____
- -
____
- -
____

Activity 12 — My Character Creation Lab

1 Character Name: _______________________________

2 What do they look like? _______________________

____

3 What is their special talent or superpower?

____

CONGRATULATIONS!

You have finished the workbook! You are an amazing writer!

SUPERSTAR WRITER

This certificate is awarded to

____

name

This award celebrates your hard work and creativity in writing.
You are a true Dyslexia Writing Star!

_____________________   _____________________

Date   Teacher/ Parent Signature

Answer Key + BONUS

Audio Included!

Writing & Coloring Mini-Book

5 fun stories with questions and coloring activities designed for young learners. Build fluency and confidence while making reading fun!

Scan the QR code to access the digital Answer Key and Bonus Mini-Book.

SCAN ME

<u>Could you spare just a minute?</u>

Watching children grow in confidence and curiosity through learning is what inspires everything we do.

That's why we care so deeply about what you think!

Even a short review, just a line or two, means more than you know. Your feedback doesn't just support our little education brand, it helps us continue creating resources with heart and purpose.

Each review is a ripple that helps us reach more young learners around the world, opening new doors in their educational journey.

And yes, it also helps keep our small business afloat so we can keep making books that matter.

Every single review fills us with gratitude and reminds us why we started this mission in the first place.